Strawberry Shortcake Characters and Designs © 1983 American Greetings Corporation. TM* designates trademarks of American
Greetings Corporation.

Library of Congress Cataloging in Publication Data: Lexau, Joan M. Strawberry Shortcake and sad Mister Sun. SUMMARY: When
the Sun feels nobody appreciates him and he spends less and less time in Strawberryland, the Strawberry kids decide they must
convince him to return.
[1. Sun—Fiction] I. Sustendal, Pat, ill.
II. Title. PZ7.L5895Ss 1983 [E] 83-8166 ISBN 0-910313-10-5
Manufactured in the United States of America 1 2 3 4 5 6 7 8 9 0

Strawberry Shortcake

and Sad Mr. Sun

Story by Joan M. Lexau
Pictures by Pat Sustendal

One summer morning Mister Sun woke up full of the grumps. He had shone brightly for days and days, but the Strawberry Kids had been so busy planting their berries that not one of them had stopped to talk to him or to say "Thank you" for the lovely weather. Mister Sun felt that nobody liked him any more.

"Rise and shine!" called a passing breeze.
"Why should I?" grumbled the Sun.
"Nobody cares if I shine or not."

He closed his eyes and went back to sleep.

Every day Mister Sun got up later and went down earlier.
He chased the sunbeams away and let the little gray clouds
cover him up.

In Strawberryland it grew colder each day.

Strawberry Shortcake shivered. "The days are so short.
The sun doesn't shine into our valley now," she said to Custard.
"My poor strawberries aren't turning red."

She went to see her neighbor, Huckleberry Pie, and his dog, Pupcake.

Huckleberry was snoozing by the Strawberry Soda Stream, his fishing pole beside him.

Strawberry woke him up. "It's so cold. We must do something," she said.

"I did do something," Huckleberry said. "I put three sweaters on."

"Let's go talk to Blueberry Muffin," Strawberry suggested.

"O.K.," said Huckleberry, closing his eyes.

"Well, let's go," Strawberry said.

"Now?" asked Huckleberry. "You mean today?" He got up slowly.

They went to see Strawberry's best friend, Blueberry Muffin.

"I'm so cold I have goose bumps!" Blueberry told them. "Some of my blueberries are turning ice blue and shrinking from all this cold."

"If it doesn't get warmer, we won't have a berry crop this year," Strawberry said. "I wonder if this could be one of the Purple Pieman's tricks."

The Kids decided to hike up to the home of the Purple Pieman, who liked to steal the Kids' berries for his pies.

Carefully they crept close to the Pieman's palace. They saw that the Purple Pieman was blowing up a big balloon with a pump. Two more balloons were tied to tall weeds.

They heard the Pieman say, "This is my last balloon, but three should be enough. Won't those Kids be surprised on their way to market! When I tie these balloons to the berry cart, their whole crop will fly off with me to Porcupine Peak. Heh, heh, heh."

He tied up the last balloon and said, "Now I'll look through my telescope and see how those berries are doing. I hope they are growing in this cold weather. Brr!"

"We'll put a stop to his silly scheme!" Strawberry said. The Kids ran to the balloons and started to untie them. Two balloons floated high in the sky. They untied the last balloon just as the Purple Pieman came running.

"Stop!" he cried. "I see what you are up to. You will ruin my lovely, naughty plan."

The Kids ran in all directions, and the last balloon's string got caught in a stickleburr bush.

"Quick! Over here!" Strawberry called.

The other Kids joined her and they all climbed up a bittersweet vine growing on a tree. They hid until the Purple Pieman gave up hunting for them.

"That was close!" Blueberry said.

"Well, we stopped the Pieman's plan," said Strawberry. "But we still don't know why the sun isn't coming to visit us any more."

"Maybe it's too much work," Huckleberry said, yawning.

Blueberry said, "Maybe the sun doesn't know just how much we need him."

"Then we'll have to let him know!" Strawberry exclaimed.

"It can't be done," said Raspberry Tart. "Mister Sun is too far away, and he's hiding behind all those clouds."

But Strawberry didn't believe in "it can't be done."

"We'll ask Orange Blossom to write a letter," she said.

Orange Blossom was indoors. Her walls were covered with beautiful pictures that she had painted.

They talked about the cold and the balloons and everything. Orange Blossom said, "Me do the letter? Somebody else could do it better. But I'll try."

Strawberry said, "I know what we can write the letter on."
She led them to a valentine tree with big heart-shaped leaves.
"When Mister Sun sees this big heart, he'll know we love him," she said.

They all pulled on a leaf while Custard and Pupcake chewed on the stem.

The leaf broke off suddenly and everyone fell down.

They took the leaf back to Orange Blossom's cottage.

She dipped her pen in a jar of concentrated blueberry juice. "What shall I write?" she asked.

Strawberry closed her eyes to think hard and said, "Begin like this:

For days and days

We've missed your warm rays."

She looked at Blueberry, who added,

"We thank you, dear sun,

For all that you've done."

Orange Blossom suggested shyly,

"It's been a trial—"

And Huckleberry shouted,

"Come back, and we'll smile!"

Orange Blossom signed it, "With love from your friends in Strawberryland." She made pictures all around it with strawberry and apricot and lime juice.

"Doesn't that smell good!" Blueberry said.

Strawberry said, "It needs one more thing. Mint Tulip can help us."

Mint Tulip was in her flower garden looking worried. "My poor Johnny-jump-ups are drooping down," she said. "My morning glories don't open up until the afternoon, and my four-o-clocks sleep all day long."

Strawberry said, "We are sending a letter to tell the sun how much we

need him. A rosebud on it would look and smell so pretty."

There was one beautiful pink rosebud left.

"Now, what will make it stick to the leaf?" Strawberry asked.

"That's easy," said Blueberry Muffin, looking down at some spots on her apron. "I had a lettuce and honey sandwich this noon. Honey is awfully sticky."

Mint Tulip attached the rosebud to the leaf.

For days, and days,
We've missed your warm rays.
We thank you, dear Sun,
For all that you've done.
It's been a trial-come
back, and we'll
smile!

The letter was ready!

"But how can we get it to the sun?" Huckleberry said.

"Balloons go up," Orange Blossom said, so softly that no one heard.

The Strawberry Kids paced back and forth, thinking hard.

Orange Blossom kept whispering, "Balloons go up."

"Balloons! That's it, Orange Blossom!" Strawberry said, giving her a hug.

They found the balloon still
stuck in the stickleburr bush.

They made sure the Pieman wasn't around,
then Strawberry stood on Huckleberry's shoulders
and reached for the balloon string.

"Don't get stuck on the stickleburr!"
Huckleberry yelled. "I don't know how
we'd get you off."

Little by little Strawberry pulled
the end of the balloon string away from
the stickleburr and carefully tied it to
the stem of the leaf letter.

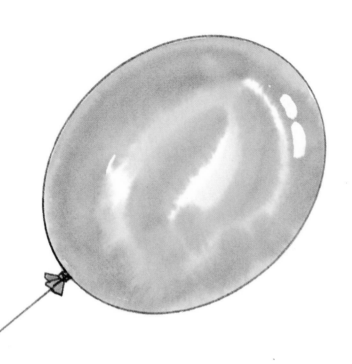

The whole string came off the stickleburr suddenly while
Strawberry was still holding onto it.

Up, up, up in the air went the balloon.

Up, up, up in the air went Strawberry.

"Help! Oh, help!" Strawberry screamed.

Lucky Bug flew off to get
a breeze to rescue her.

The breeze puffed
and pushed the balloon
near the ground.

But the balloon bounced
around and bobbed this
way and that.

"Strawberry, catch my fishing line!" Huckleberry yelled.

He cast the line as high as he could. Strawberry caught it. All the Kids helped get her down on the ground.

"Oh, my! I feel all skitter-skattered," Strawberry said.

The balloon sailed away high in the sky. Soon they couldn't see it any more.

"Do you think it will reach the sun?" Orange Blossom whispered.

"We all have to wish hard," Strawberry said.

The Strawberry Kids held hands in a circle
and wished with all their might.

The balloon floated up and up through the little gray clouds, high over the world.

As it neared the sun, it grew hotter and hotter.

Finally it exploded—P O P—before it got to Mr. Sun.

The leaf began to flutter back down toward the world.

Mister Sun took a deep breath and bellowed, "BRING ME
THAT HEART-SHAPED NOTE!"

A little breeze brought the leaf to him.

"It says, 'Thank you.' Nobody has said that to me before!" said Mister Sun. "It says they need me. It says love from my friends! And it's all on a beautiful heart! Oh, my, I feel so warm all over!"

The next morning Mister Sun rose early. He told the little gray clouds to go away, and he sailed as fast as he could to the sky over Strawberryland.

He shone down all day, making everyone warm and cozy. The berries and flowers quickly perked up and began to grow.

All the Strawberry Kids had a Sunshine Party.

A cloud rained a gentle rain. Just enough so the berries and flowers had a refreshing drink of water.

Even while it rained, the sun kept on shining.

"Look!" Orange Blossom said. "Did you ever see such a beautiful rainbow?"

"I think," said Strawberry Shortcake, "that lovely things usually happen when we remember to say thanks."